CAVE OF THE BOOKWORMS

BY MICHAEL DAHL
ILLUSTRATED BY BRADFORD KENDALL

Librarian Reviewer
Laurie K. Holland
Media Specialist (National Board Certified), Edina, MN
MA in Elementary Education, Minnesota State University, Mankato

Reading Consultant
Elizabeth Stedem
Educator/Consultant, Colorado Springs, CO
MA in Elementary Education, University of Denver, CO

STONE ARCH BOOKS
Minneapolis   San Diego

Zone Books are published by Stone Arch Books,
A Capstone Imprint
1710 Roe Crest Drive
North Mankato, Minnesota 56003
www.capstonepub.com

Library of Congress Cataloging-in-Publication Data
Dahl, Michael.
    Cave of the Bookworms / by Michael Dahl; illustrated by
Bradford Kendall.
    p. cm. — (Zone Books - Library of Doom)
    ISBN 978-1-4342-0489-9 (library binding)
    ISBN 978-1-4342-0549-0 (paperback)
    [1. Books and reading—Fiction. 2. Librarians—Fiction.
3. Fantasy.] I. Kendall, Bradford, ill. II. Title.
PZ7.D15134Cav 2008
[Fic]—dc22   2007032220

Summary: One night, after awakening from a terrible dream, a
young boy heads out on his bike. Soon he arrives at a mysterious
cave, which he feels an urge explore. Inside, a giant, deadly worm
has trapped the Librarian! Now, the boy is in danger as well.

Creative Director: Heather Kindseth
Senior Designer for Cover and Interior: Kay Fraser
Graphic Designer: Brann Garvey

Printed in the United States of America in Stevens Point, Wisconsin.
012013
007118R

TABLE OF CONTENTS

The Library of Doom is the world's largest collection of strange and dangerous books. The Librarian's duty is to keep the books from falling into the hands of those who would use them for evil purposes.

CHAPTER 1

THE DARK DREAM

Deep in the night, a young boy dreams.

He dreams about a strange man, **fighting** nightmare creatures.

Giant worms surround the man.

They open their terrible mouths.

The boy wakes up, shouting.

Quickly, he goes to his bedroom

window and looks out.

Moonlight touches his bicycle.

For some reason, the boy wants to go for a ride.

He feels like he **has to.**

CHAPTER 2

DOWN THE HOLE

The boy rides his bike down the **long path** from his house.

He pedals through gloomy
woods.

Dark branches seem to reach
toward him from every side.

Suddenly, the boy `stops.`

The place reminds him of
something from his dreams.

The boy travels **deeper** into the woods.

He does not know where he is going.

Soon, the boy sees a dark shape
in the ground.

It is a **gigantic hole.**

The boy begins to **climb** down the deep hole.

He does not know why.

CHAPTER 3

THE CAVE

The boy climbs deeper and deeper into the hole.

A strange light **glows** at the bottom of the hole.

It is coming from a giant cave.

The boy has seen this cave before in his dreams.

Suddenly, the boy sees
something else from his dreams.

A giant worm!

The worm is building a `sticky web` in the center of the cave.

In the middle of the web, a man struggles. He is `trapped!`

In the dim light of the cave, the boy sees shapes next to the man.

The shapes are round, like `eggs.`

CHAPTER 4

FOOD FOR WORMS

The boy **realizes** these are the worm's eggs.

The eggs surround the man in the web.

The boy has seen something like this before.

In his **books**, the boy has read about insects laying their eggs.

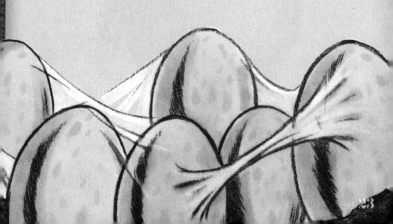

When the eggs **hatch**, the young creatures need food.

The man will become food for the **worm's babies**.

CHAPTER 5

THE BOOK LIGHT

The giant worm **turns** and looks at the boy.

The boy steps back quickly. He hears a `clink` on the `ground`.

It is his book light. It **fell** off his t-shirt.

The boy grabs the book light and aims it at the worm.

The **beam hits** the worm in the face.

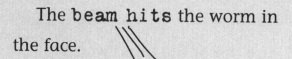

The worm is **blinded.** Its scream echoes through the cave.

Its giant body thrashes back and forth. Its giant tail crushes the eggs.

The tail of the blind worm **swings** near the boy.

The boy falls to the ground and drops his light.

The web has been ripped apart by the struggling worm.

The man is **free.**

"Who are you?" asks the boy.

"I am the Librarian," says the man. "You have saved me."

"I was **exploring** this cave when the bookworm trapped me.

This cave is very close to my library."

"Where is your library?" asks the boy. "May I see it?"

Suddenly, the hungry bookworm rises up.

It **lunges** at the boy, opening its terrible mouth.

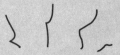

The boy **wakes up**, shouting.

He was having a dream.

But when he puts his hand to his chest, his book light is **gone.**

THE END

A PAGE FROM THE LIBRARY OF DOOM

MORE ABOUT BOOKWORMS

Bookworms do exist! They are sometimes the **larva**, or worm-like young, of a fully-grown insect. The larva from more than 150 different kinds of beetles can damage books by eating paper or boring through covers. Here are some creepy examples of real-life library foes.

Dermestid (dur-MES-tid) beetles are scavengers that feed on skin. Museums use them to clean animal skeletons! Some dermestids attack the leather bindings of old books. Remember, leather is skin, too.

Drugstore beetles have sharp, saw-like antennae. They like to feed on books. They also bore through wood and can be found digging their way into library shelves. A single female drugstore beetle produces as many as 800,000 descendents a year!

An insect with the amazing name **Anobium punctatum** (uh-NO-bee-um punk-TAH-toom) lays its eggs on the edges of books. The hatchlings, looking like worms, burrow into the books hunting for food. They feed on microscopic fungus that grows on dark, moist pages.

The **powder-post beetle** bores into bookshelves. It chews holes in the wood and then packs them full with a soft, powdery dust. When most of the supporting wood has been chewed up, the shelves will eventually collapse. Timber!

ABOUT THE AUTHOR

Michael Dahl is the author of more than 100 books for children and young adults. He has twice won the AEP Distinguished Achievement Award for his nonfiction. His Finnegan Zwake mystery series was chosen by the Agatha Awards to be among the five best mystery books for children in 2002 and 2003. He collects books on poison and graveyards, and lives in a haunted house in Minneapolis, Minnesota.

ABOUT THE ILLUSTRATOR

Bradford Kendall has enjoyed drawing for as long as he can remember. As a boy, he loved to read comic books and watch old monster movies. He graduated from the Rhode Island School of Design with a BFA in Illustration. He has owned his own commercial art business since 1983, and lives in Providence, Rhode Island, with his wife, Leigh, and their two children Lily and Stephen. They also have a cat named Hansel and a dog named Gretel.

GLOSSARY

creatures (KREE-churz)—strange, unusual types of animals

echoes (EK-ohz)—sound repeated when it reflects off the walls of a large room; yell into a cave and your voice **echoes** back at you.

exploring (ek-SPLOR-ing)—traveling in a new area for adventure or discovery

gigantic (jye-GAN-tik)—really, really big

gloomy (GLOO-mee)—dark and creepy

thrashes (THRASH-ez)—moves about wildly and violently

DISCUSSION QUESTIONS

1. The boy saves the Librarian from the giant bookworm. Does this make his decision to leave the house alone at night okay? Why or why not?

2. The boy could have been hurt trying to save the Librarian. Would you risk being hurt to save someone you didn't know? Explain your answer.

3. At the end of the story, the boy realizes he was only dreaming. But then, he discovers his book light is missing. Do you think his adventure was a dream or real? Explain your answer.

WRITING PROMPTS

1. The reader never finds out why the Librarian was exploring the bookworm's cave. Write a story explaining why he was inside the cave and what he was searching for.

2. Scary dreams can often seem very real. Describe the creepiest dream you've ever had. What made it so scary?

3. The young boy saved the Librarian's life. But what would have happened if the boy hadn't shown up just in time? Write a new ending to the story, where the Librarian must get out of the web alone.